Dear Parent:

Your child's love of reading starts here!

Every child learns to read in a different way and at his or her own speed. Some go back and forth between reading levels and read favorite books again and again. Others read through each level in order. You can help your young reader improve and become more confident by encouraging his or her own interests and abilities. From books your child reads with you to the first books he or she reads alone, there are I Can Read Books for every stage of reading:

SHARED READING
Basic language, word repetition, and whimsical illustrations, ideal for sharing with your emergent reader

BEGINNING READING
Short sentences, familiar words, and simple concepts for children eager to read on their own

READING WITH HELP
Engaging stories, longer sentences, and language play for developing readers

READING ALONE
Complex plots, challenging vocabulary, and high-interest topics for the independent reader

I Can Read Books have introduced children to the joy of reading since 1957. Featuring award-winning authors and illustrators and a fabulous cast of beloved characters, I Can Read Books set the standard for beginning readers.

A lifetime of discovery begins with the magical words "I Can Read!"

Visit www.icanread.com for information
on enriching your child's reading experience.

The Berenstain Bears Share and Share Alike!
Copyright © 2022 by Berenstain Publishing, Inc.
All rights reserved. Printed in the United States of America.
No part of this book may be used or reproduced in any manner whatsoever without written permission except
in the case of brief quotations embodied in critical articles and reviews. For information address HarperCollins
Children's Books, a division of HarperCollins Publishers, 195 Broadway, New York, NY 10007.
www.icanread.com

Library of Congress Control Number: 2021943547
ISBN 978-0-06-302453-3 (trade bdg.) — ISBN 978-0-06-302452-6 (pbk.)

22 23 24 25 26 LSCC 10 9 8 7 6 5 4 3 2 1 ❖ First Edition

1 BEGINNING READING **I Can Read!**

The Berenstain Bears®

Share & Share Alike!

Mike Berenstain

**Based on the characters created by
Stan and Jan Berenstain**

HARPER
An Imprint of HarperCollinsPublishers

It's summer in Bear Country.

It is very hot!

Brother, Sister, and Honey

splash in their little pool.

It is nice and cool!

Papa watches the cubs
cool off in their little pool.
He wants to cool off, too.
But he is too big to share
the cubs' little pool.

"We need a bigger pool!" says Papa.

"I will get a bigger pool!"

Papa buys a new pool.

He sets it up.

He fills it with water.

The big pool is now ready.

Papa gets in.

"Ah!" he says.

"It is nice and cool!"

"Oh boy!" say the cubs.

"A bigger pool! Let's jump in!"

The cubs jump into the bigger pool.

"Wait a minute!" says Papa.

"You have your own little pool.

This pool is for me!"

"Now, Papa!" says Mama.

"Don't be selfish!

Remember, share and share alike!"

Papa knows Mama is right.

He shares the big pool with the cubs.

The cubs laugh and play
in the big pool.
They splash and jump.
They splash on Papa.
They jump on Papa.

"This is fun!" says Sister.

"This is a great pool!"

"Yes," says Brother.

"We should not keep it to ourselves.

We should share it with others."

"Share the pool with others?"
asks Papa.

"Yes!" says Sister.

"We should share it with all our
friends."

"But then there won't be
enough room for me!" says Papa.

"Now, Papa!" says Brother.

"Don't be selfish!"

"Remember," says Sister,

"share and share alike!"

Papa knows they are right.

The cubs invite all their

friends to share the pool.

Soon lots of cubs

are swimming in the pool.

They laugh and play.

They splash and jump.

There is no room for Papa.

"Don't worry, Papa!"
says Mama. "Now you can
have the cubs' little pool
all to yourself."
"Oh boy," says Papa.

Papa sits in the cubs' little pool.

He runs the hose over his head
to cool off.

All the cubs splash and play
in the big pool.

"As I always say," says Papa, sighing, "share and share alike!"